THE ADVENTURES OF "CHUCK E. BEAVER" AND FRIENDS

CHRISTMAS COMES TO THE FOREST

Written by
Kiki

Illustrated by
ROBERT ELLIOTT
and
RON MIGLIORE

Published by
Montbec Inc.

Publisher
MATT ARENY

Publication Advisor
JOSE AZEVEDO

Editorial Supervisor
ETHEL SALTZMAN

Artwork Supervisor
PIERRE RENAUD

ISBN 2-89227-210-6

CHRISTMAS COMES TO THE FOREST

It was wintertime in the forest and beautiful thick snow covered the trees and ground everywhere.

Winter was the season that Chuck E. liked best. It meant that Christmas would soon be here, and that meant lots of wonderful presents and good food.

Chuck E. loved to receive presents and he looked forward to this every year. This particular Christmas would be a bit different from all of the other Christmases Chuck E. had experienced. This Christmas would be a very special one. One that would teach Chuck E. what Christmas was all about.

It was December 23rd, just two days before Christmas, and everyone was busy preparing for the big day. Chuck E. and his dad were out busily searching for a Christmas tree. It had to be big enough to hold all of the many presents Chuck E. would receive.

"Hey, Pop, this one looks like a good one over here!" Chuck E. shouted as he pointed out a large tree on the Christmas tree lot.

"Yes, son, I think that one will do just fine!" Mr. Beaver agreed with a smile.

"Do you think Santa Claus will bring me lots of presents this year, Dad?" Chuck E. asked.

"Well, have you been a good boy this year?" Mr. Beaver asked in return.

"I always try my best, Pop!" Chuck E. responded proudly.

"Well, then I think Santa won't forget you on Christmas Day," Mr. Beaver assured Chuck E.

"Oh boy, I can hardly wait!" Chuck E. exclaimed with excitement.

As Mr. Beaver was tying down the
Christmas tree to the top of the car,
Chuck E. noticed a young beaver with
tattered clothes standing in the snow,
staring with a sad expression at the many
Christmas trees remaining on the lot.

"Gee, Dad, do you see that kid over there?" Chuck E. asked curiously. "I wonder why he looks so sad this close to Christmas?"

"I don't know, son, but he sure looks like he could use a friend right now," Mr. Beaver replied. "Why don't you go over and see if he needs any help?"

"Okay, Pop," Chuck E. replied with enthusiasm. "I'll do my best!"

As Chuck E. was making his way towards
him, the youngster suddenly noticed
Chuck E. approaching and he ran away.
Chuck E. yelled for him to stop, but the
boy continued to run faster. Chuck E.
realized he couldn't catch up with him, so
he stopped and headed back to the car.

"Gee, Pop, he just ran away," Chuck E. told his dad. "I hope he didn't think I was going to hurt him," Chuck E. added.

"Maybe he did, son," Mr. Beaver said. "But don't feel too bad. You know you were only trying to help."

"I know, Dad, but I still can't help wondering if something was really wrong," Chuck E. worried.

"I know how you feel, son," Mr. Beaver said consolingly. "There are a lot of people who are less fortunate than we are, and that is why we should always be thankful for what we have."

"Do you mean that maybe he was sad because he might not be having a Christmas tree or any presents this year?" Chuck E. asked.

"That could be true, son," Mr. Beaver replied. "For some people Christmas doesn't bring any presents," Mr. Beaver continued.

"No presents! I couldn't imagine Christmas without a Christmas tree or any presents," Chuck E. said in disbelief. "It sure would be nice if we could give him something."

"That's a nice thought, son," Mr. Beaver replied. "Maybe we could invite him and his family to share Christmas Day with us?" he suggested.

"Boy! Do you think we could, Dad?" Chuck E. asked with excitement. "I'd hate to think of them spending Christmas without anything to enjoy."

"If it means that much to you, Chuck E., then I don't think your mom would mind at all," Mr. Beaver said. "But we're going to have to find him first so that we know where his family lives."

"Say, Pop, why don't we come back here tomorrow," Chuck E. suggested. "I'll bet he'll be here looking at the trees again."

"Alright, son," Mr. Beaver agreed. "That's probably our best chance of finding him."

So Chuck E. and his father went home to tell Mrs. Beaver of their plans. Mrs. Beaver thought it was a nice idea as well, and praised Chuck E. for being so generous.

The next day didn't come quickly enough for Chuck E. It was Christmas Eve and Chuck E. and his parents had only one day to find the young beaver and his family before Christmas was here. This now meant more to Chuck E. than receiving his presents.

"Dad, can we go to the tree lot now and see if he's there?" Chuck E. asked impatiently.

"Alright, son, but I don't want you to get your hopes up too high," Mr. Beaver cautioned. "He might not show up. In fact, we might not see him again."

"He'll be there. I know it!" Chuck E. said with confidence.

Chuck E. and his dad quickly headed off to the tree lot. When they got there they decided to stay in the warm car until the youngster showed up. They were there for almost an hour when Mr. Beaver suggested they go home.

"Oh, please, Dad, just five more minutes," Chuck E. pleaded. "I'm sure he'll be here."

"Alright, son, but if he isn't here in five minutes we'll have to go home," Mr. Beaver stated.

"Okay," Chuck E. agreed grudgingly.

The five minutes were almost up when Chuck E. noticed the young beaver again standing near the fence.

"There he is, Pop!" Chuck E. shouted with joy.

"Wait, son, he might run away again if you run over there," Mr. Beaver replied. "Why don't I come with you this time and you can call out to him first."

"Alright, Pop," Chuck E. agreed, but as Chuck E. and his dad stepped out of the car and moved towards the young boy, he became nervous once again and bolted away.

"Oh no, Pop!" Chuck E. exclaimed. "We'll never catch up to him now!"

"Maybe the tree lot owner knows who he is and where he lives," Mr. Beaver suggested with hope.

Chuck E. and his dad walked quickly to the tree lot office and asked the owner if he knew the young beaver. The owner did know him and he told them about him and his family.

"Oh, yes," the lot owner replied, "he's the Beaverson boy. Sad story! You see, his father has been very ill for some time and can't work. His mother has to look after his father all of the time so she can't work either," he explained.

"Do you know where they live?" Mr. Beaver inquired.

"Yes, they live in a run-down house on Old Mill Road," the lot owner replied. "I don't even know if they have enough firewood for the winter."

"Come on, Pop, lets go there!" Chuck E. begged.

"Alright, son, it's the least we can do," Mr. Beaver agreed.

But while Chuck E. and his father were on their way to the Beaversons' house, Chuck E. thought of a better way to make their Christmas a little more special.

"Pop, why don't we get all of our friends together and bring Christmas to the Beaversons!" Chuck E. proposed.

"What do you mean, son?" Mr. Beaver asked, somewhat puzzled.

"Well, what they need most is a clean, warm house, some good food and loving friends, right?" Chuck E. stated. "If we all pitch in, we could give them all of that!"

"I think you've got something there, son!" Mr. Beaver exclaimed proudly. "We'll make this a Christmas they'll never forget!"

"Okay, let's get started!" Chuck E. said enthusiastically.

Chuck E. and his dad quickly drove home and explained the idea to Mrs. Beaver. She got all of the mothers together that night and everyone took part. Some helped with the cooking, others fixed up some old clothing to bring, while Chuck E. and his friends put together enough money to buy a small Christmas tree.

All of the fathers gathered up their tools and materials so that they could start fixing up the Beaversons' house. Then they began cutting firewood. The parents worked feverishly into the night, so that everything would be ready for Christmas Day. Morning came soon and Chuck E. ran to wake up his parents right away.

"Mom, Pop, come on, we have to hurry and go over to the Beaversons!" Chuck E. exclaimed.

"But, son, don't you even want to open up your presents first?" Mr. Beaver asked.

"That can wait, Pop!" Chuck E. replied earnestly. "The most important thing right now is to make sure the Beaversons have the Christmas they deserve!"

"Okay, son, let's call the others so we can all go over together," Mr. Beaver suggested.

Mr. Beaver called all of the other families, and they were just as eager as Chuck E. to go over to the Beaversons. Chuck E. and his parents quickly gathered all of the things they were bringing and headed over to the Chipmunks' house where the others were waiting.

Once they had all arrived, they made
their way over to the Beaversons.
As each car stopped in front of the
Beaversons' house, they gathered up all
of the gifts and materials they had
brought and went up to the front door.

Instead of knocking, Chuck E. suggested that they all join in and sing a special Christmas carol. Soon everyone was singing loudly, "We wish you a Merry Christmas, We wish you a Merry Christmas!"

It wasn't long before Mrs. Beaverson came to see what all the noise was about. She peered through the window of the front door to see a most beautiful sight. She quickly called for her son and husband to join her. As they listened to the singing, they held each other tight and tears of joy streamed down their faces.

The Beaversons soon opened the door and asked everyone to come in. Chuck E. and his parents were the first ones to greet them as Chuck E. presented them with the little Christmas tree he and his friends had decorated.

Young Billy Beaverson noticed Chuck E. and remembered him from the tree lot the other night.

"It's you!" Billy said with bewilderment. "I thought you were chasing me away from the lot!"

"Oh no," Chuck E. responded. "We saw how much you admired them and just wanted you to have one!"

"This is the best Christmas ever!" Billy shouted with joy. Chuck E. just smiled and thought to himself, it sure is.

Christmas is more than just presents

Waiting under the tree.

It's all about loving and giving

The way the whole world should be!

Your friend,
Chuck E.